Quick, Go Peek!

Written by Joëlle Murphy • Illustrated by Slug Signorino

Good Year Books

I wonder what happens
to the food in my refrigerator
when I close the door.

Does the salad bowl?
I wonder . . . .
Quick, go peek!

Aha!

4

Does the ice scream?
I wonder . . . .
Quick, go peek!

Aha!

Does the lamb chop?
I wonder . . . .
Quick, go peek!

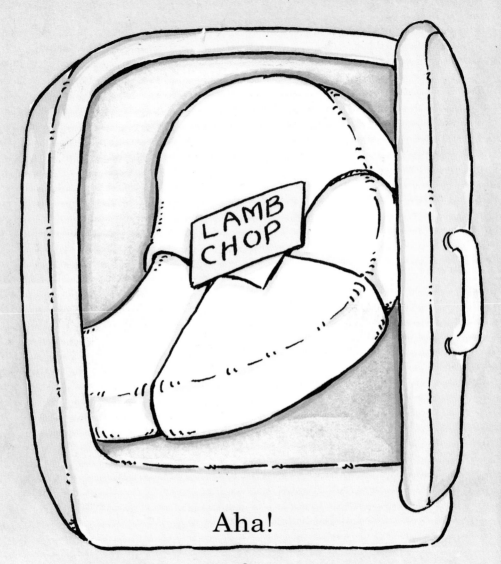

Aha!

Does the milk shake?
I wonder . . . .
Quick, go peek!

Aha!

Does the egg roll?
I wonder . . . .
Quick, go peek!

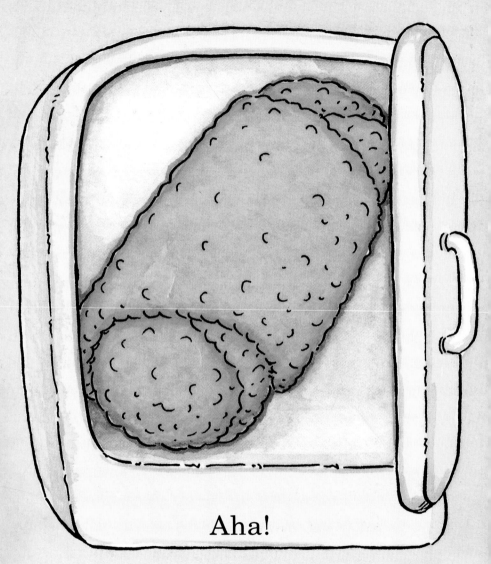

Aha!

Does the banana split?
I wonder . . . .
Quick, go peek!

Aha!

Does the refrigerator run?

Quick, go catch it!